To my family

A Christmas of Surprises

~A Novella~

by
Derek L. Polen

Goal Line Group LLC

Copyright © 2019 by Goal Line Group LLC

All rights reserved. No part of this publication may be reproduced, stored in a retrieval system, or transmitted by any means – electronic, mechanical, photographic (photocopying), recording, or otherwise – without prior permission in writing from the author.

This book is a work of fiction. Names, characters, businesses, places, events, locales, and incidents are either the products of the author's imagination or used in a fictitious manner. Any resemblance to actual events, organizations, locales, businesses, or actual persons, living or dead, is purely coincidental. The author and publisher shall have no liability or responsibility to any person or entity regarding loss or damage incurred, or alleged to have incurred, directly or indirectly, by the information contained in this book. Any trademarked names used in this book are for editorial context with no intention of infringement of that trademark.

ISBN-13: 978-1-7335651-6-5

TABLE OF CONTENTS

Tis the Season to be Stressed	1
The Clock is Ticking	7
Gift Game Plan	13
Wild Pitch	19
Thanksgiving	25
Black Friday	35
The Joyful Drummer	49
Spiritually Fed	55
Wild Goose Chase	67
Homerun Surprise	77
A Surprise Encounter	85
The Christmas Program	93
Gingerbread Festival	97
The Blitz	105
Christmas Blessing	111
Full of Surprises	117
Christmas Morning	123
Putting Christmas in Perspective	129

Tis the Season to be Stressed

What do you think of when you hear the word "Christmas"? Many people will think about the joyful memories they have from personal experiences with family and friends, or from those lovely Hollywood "feel good" scenes in movies. These memories may include attending a candlelight service at church, listening to an amazing chorus of carolers singing, driving around town with your family looking at Christmas lights, or watching your favorite holiday movie with the people you love most. During Christmas we enjoy many other holiday traditions, spend time with family, put up festive decorations, and enjoy baking a mountain of delicious treats (or some of us are just on the consuming end of those treats).

There are typically two types of people when it comes to Christmas time. On one side of the spectrum are the ones who really embrace it and get fully immersed in the holiday. Or, the other type who get stressed out about it and are ready for it to be over. Those who love it are already adding peppermint to their coffee in October and have been watching Christmas movies since the day after Halloween. For the people who do not get as jazzed up about Christmas, their stress levels increase at the mere mention of the word Christmas. This is a story about Noah, who usually fell on the side of "bring on the peppermint and let's watch a Christmas movie tonight", until the past couple years.

From his childhood, Noah could remember looking at Christmas lights with his family, participating in Christmas programs, and the fun, but drama-filled family gatherings. Twenty years later he could still smell and taste his Aunt Celia May's homemade peppermint fudge. He could also remember when his big brother, Michael, and he would make the living room look like a tornado hit it after they opened up their Christmas presents.

During his childhood, every Christmas was a good Christmas for Noah. His parents always tried hard to give him and his brother a wonderful Christmas. Noah knew his parents were not wealthy and he was grateful for the efforts his parents put into giving him and Michael a special Christmas.

When Noah met his wife, Gracelyn, Christmas became more special to him since he had her to share it with. After they got married, they started their own traditions. A few years into the marriage when Noah and Gracelyn had their children, Emma and Liam, it really fueled his Christmas spirit. Having his children to buy for and share traditions with made the Christmas season more special to him.

Christmas time for Noah was full of happy memories, but over the last few years he did not enjoy the holiday season like he had most of his life. Noah was extremely career-focused. The further he climbed the corporate ladder the more focused on his career he became. He always wanted to please his boss and his employees, and he had difficulty saying no to tasks thrown his way at work.

Last year his employer went through an acquisition at the end of the year and Noah missed out on so much during the holidays. They skipped the Gingerbread Festival because he had to work and because of a work emergency he missed out on his children's Christmas program.

He felt bad to some degree, but still kept his career a top priority.

The holidays were not the only thing that Noah's work impacted. Noah proclaimed himself a Christian, but rarely went to church. It was a common theme throughout the year that he never went to church because Sunday morning was when he would catch up from his sleep deprived days before.

With the work demands and his unbalanced work and home life, Noah was missing so much of the precious moments of his kids growing up. He would miss out on certain school events and was not able to help coach his kids' sports teams. Noah knew he was missing out on things, but he did not want to fail at work and wanted to provide the best he could for his family. His career was taking front seat to many things in his family's life and over the recent Christmas seasons it had put a damper on his Christmas spirit.

The Clock is Ticking

When Halloween approaches it seems to Noah that the days on the calendar kick into overdrive. Before you know it Thanksgiving is here and then Christmas is knocking on the door. Time seems to move at a supersonic speed and there are a million things to accomplish during this chaotic time of the year.

During the holidays Noah's family would have their children's Christmas programs, winter sports schedules, office Christmas parties, gatherings with family and friends, travel to see family, and more. While all this was enjoyable for Noah (well most of it was) and time consuming, he left most of the scheduling up to Gracelyn. He would attend as much as he could, but with his job getting first priority over his time, he always had to miss out on a few events.

When he would be home at night, he was there physically, but mentally he was somewhere else. He could never totally turn off work mode in his mind. One night as the family was watching their favorite television series, and Noah was working on his laptop while half engaged in the program, he went through his daily "how was school" routine.

"So, how was school today?" Noah asked while still staring at his computer.

"It was fine. We're working on our multiplication and Mrs. Warner is making us read some long chapter book that's not very exciting," said Liam.

"Well you know reading is important and sometimes we have to read books we don't always like. Don't let that discourage you from reading other things too," replied Noah.

"We're working on our Christmas program songs too," Liam said with excitement.

"They are really good songs," added Emma, "Our class is helping with the set decorations."

Noah nodded like he was hearing everything they were saying, but continued to look at his computer as he was focused on something very important. It was at that moment, Liam would ask Noah something that quickly shifted his focus away from his work.

"So, Dad, do you think you can come to our Christmas programs this year? Everyone else's parents come to it. Or do you think you'll have to work again?"

"Um, I'm sorry buddy. You know I want to try and be there. I'm sorry I missed last year," said Noah.

"Dad, maybe we can go to the Gingerbread Festival this year too, like we used to," added Emma.

That was the light bulb moment for Noah as an extreme feeling of guilt poured over him. He was in shock. Just like that, those few words from his children made him feel like a terrible father. It was not their fault. They were just asking simple questions. He realized that this Christmas he wanted to make up for being so focused on his work.

When Emma asked about the Gingerbread Festival, that was the one thing that Noah's family cherished every year for several years and had become a family tradition until last year. He was an old fashioned guy who appreciated the value of having family traditions. In his mind, these traditions created wonderful memories for his family and it gave them something to look forward to every year. However, last year he blew it by going on a work trip during the festival, so they did not get to go.

Noah decided it was time to double down. In addition to finding more time to spend with his family, Noah wanted to step up his game with the gift buying this year. This year was going to be different all the way around. He challenged himself to get everyone close to him a gift that would show he put more effort and thoughtfulness into their gift this Christmas. This year the gifts he gave would show how much he cared.

To try to spend time with his family, Noah set a goal of taking vacation days a few days prior to Christmas, plus the whole week between Christmas and New Year's Day. With Thanksgiving Day approaching, it was time for Noah to get his Christmas list and to-do's in order...and the clock was ticking.

Gift Game Plan

It was the Sunday before Thanksgiving and Noah thought it would be a good opportunity to start jotting down some ideas on what to buy everyone for Christmas. With all the Black Friday sales approaching he wanted to develop his Christmas gift game plan. Noah pulled out his laptop and created a spreadsheet that would have all the names of everyone he needed to purchase a Christmas gift for. Each person would have a list of practical or fun things he thought they would like or had requested. There was also a "Wow" gift category he added for each person. This would be that gift that he thought would make the person say "Wow!" when they saw it.

After several moments pondering what to get Gracelyn, the idea came to him. When Noah met Gracelyn she told him about this painting she came across when she was in college. She had been on vacation with her parents in the Smoky Mountains when they went into one of the gift shops. In the shop she discovered this painting that she would never forget. It was a beautiful painting of the inside of a church with an eagle rising out of it. The painting had one person inside praying and ornate woodwork throughout the church. Traditional wooden pews, vibrant stained glass windows, and the bible verse of Isaiah 40:31 completed the picture. The inspiring verse was at the bottom of the painting and it read, "...but those who hope in the Lord will renew their strength. They will soar on wings like eagles; they will run and not grow weary, they will walk and not be faint."

As a college student, Gracelyn did not have enough money to buy the painting for herself. She really wanted it, but never mentioned it to her parents since she did not think they would get it for her because it cost too much. To this day, Gracelyn always remembered the painting and how it had this spiritual impact on her.

Noah remembered her talking about the painting a few times during their marriage and this was the year he was going track it down.

Feeling good about the gift he was going to try and get Gracelyn, Noah started putting down ideas for their kids, Emma and Liam. When Noah's kids were born his love for Christmas deepened because he had these amazing children to share Christmas with. Christmas time became more special for him because his kids gave him more enjoyment than he could ever imagine.

This year Emma and Liam were 12 and 8 years old. With four years in between them both, along with them being a girl and a boy, they usually had different ideas for their Christmas wish list. Emma usually wanted something music, sports, or clothing related. Liam loved anything that pertained to gaming, movies, or technology. Luckily, Liam still believed in Santa, so Noah was able to continue to keep that Christmas magic alive. Not having any common interests between them, it was difficult to get them a gift that they would both enjoy, however this Christmas introduced a new item the whole family would enjoy.

Every holiday season, articles are published or news segments on television would feature the "Hottest Toys of the Season". These popular toys would often create the challenge of availability. Of all the highly coveted toys over recent years, this year had the biggest of them all. It was the year of the C.H.A.M.P. Robot.

The C.H.A.M.P. Robot was pretty amazing. Emma and Liam would always comment how cool the robot was when they would see a commercial about it, and Noah and Gracelyn even wanted one for themselves. He knew that the kids, actually the entire family, would enjoy it very much. The problem was there was a limited supply of them and everyone in the world wanted one.

The C.H.A.M.P. Robot had really unique features and would even make you feel like it was part of the family. It played music, projected movies onto a wall, and played basic games like trivia with you. In addition to those features, it could even help you with your homework. If the kids had any questions, they could ask the robot and it would guide them along a path to finding a solution, without just spitting out an answer. The robot had facial recognition and artificial intelligence that allowed it to constantly gain more knowledge and carry on conversations with people. The C.H.A.M.P. Robot was a robot toy like no other.

Part of the complexity of getting this toy, in addition to the fact that there were a limited number of them manufactured, was that you had to get it in the store. Otherwise, you would pay three times the retail price at an online auction site. Noah was pretty conservative when it came to spending money and paying three times what something was worth was not something he was prepared to do. He decided to tackle the challenge of visiting every store in a one hour radius to find the highly sought after toy. Noah continued to plug in some gift ideas in the spreadsheet, but he knew that for a few people it would take some more thinking about what to get them. Over the next few days he would finish up his thoughtful and challenging gift idea game plan.

Wild Pitch

"So, what time do you plan on getting home tonight?" Gracelyn asked Noah as he was finishing his breakfast.

"Since we are off for Thanksgiving tomorrow, I'll probably be a little later tonight. We have a bunch of reports to submit to the executive team," replied Noah, "I'll do my best to be home by dinner."

Gracelyn knew Noah was stressed and felt bad for him, so she did what she did best and gave him some encouraging words, "I'm proud of you hon. You work so hard to provide for our family. I know you don't want to be in the office any longer than you have to. Don't get too stressed out. We'll have Thanksgiving break tomorrow and a much longer break at Christmas."

Gracelyn gave him a huge kiss as he headed out the door to go to work.

As Noah was heading into work, he started thinking about what he would get his boss, Hank, for Christmas. In the past, Noah would get a small gift from his travels abroad. When he visited another country he would always take time to venture out to a local marketplace and shop in all the unique stores. Noah loved doing this since he would get to experience the local culture. This was his opportunity to get really good gifts and mementos for his family...and his boss.

Noah had a really good relationship with his boss, Hank. Even though Hank was his boss, he was also a friend. Noah started at the company a year after Hank did and Hank helped teach Noah the ropes. They shared many similar interests like sports and music. There was a close level of trust between the two of them.

During the last couple years, the company was very demanding on both of them. Hank was the type of boss to stick up for his employees. He also rolled up his sleeves and got in the trenches with the team. It was these type of actions that Noah gained so much respect for him.

From last year's trip to Germany, Noah brought back a miniature cuckoo clock for his boss. The year prior, he was doing work in China and got his boss a hand carved terracotta army chess set. For all the work Hank had done for

Noah, he decided he wanted to do something special, but he was not quite sure what that special Christmas gift would be.

It was near the end of the day and one of Noah's colleagues stopped by his office to ask, "So, what gift from your travels abroad are you getting Hank for Christmas this year?"

"Well, I haven't decided yet. I didn't travel anywhere different this year and have been pretty much here the whole time consumed with these projects. To be honest, I'm struggling with a good idea this year," replied Noah.

Trying to help brainstorm ideas, the colleague suggested, "You know....he does like to collect sports memorabilia. Maybe there's an autograph you could get him."

It was at that moment, the gift idea for Hank hit Noah like a wild pitch. Noah knew Hank had been a catcher for the Kingstown State University Knights baseball team. Noah thought how cool it would be if they had any remnants of the time period that Hank played there. Something from Hank's baseball glory days would be a perfect fit for his collection. Noah was not sure what they might have, but he was determined that this was the right direction to get Hank that "wow factor" gift.

Thanksgiving

It was Thanksgiving Day and for Noah this time of year was when his stress and anxiety really kicked in. He had the car all packed up and ready to go. He and his family were on their way to a two hour journey to Gracelyn's Aunt Lucille and Uncle Walt's annual Thanksgiving feast. The Thanksgiving dinner with Gracelyn's family was usually an enjoyable time as it kicked off the holiday season.

During the drive, Gracelyn got out her pen and paper and started writing down Christmas ideas. The kids had their headphones on, so they did not hear anything. Plus, Noah and Gracelyn talked in code when it was an idea for one of the kids.

"So, any ideas on what to get your parents?" asked Gracelyn.

"I haven't got a clue," replied Noah, "I'll have to keep giving it some thought."

Over the next few moments, Noah would think about what special gift he would get for his parents, John and Doris.

Family was so important to his parents and they always cherished handmade gifts from the kids. Having "family" and "handmade by the kids" in mind, Noah decided on an easy to make, yet meaningful gift for his parents.

"What do you think about this idea for mom and dad?" Noah asked Gracelyn, "I noticed someone at work had something similar in their office. We could do a collage of pictures bordered by handprints of our family and also include Michael. Childhood pictures of he and I, plus a bunch of our family, and if you add our handprints on the outside, I think they would just love it."

"That's a terrific idea!" said Gracelyn, "Here's something else I just thought. Building on the family idea, we can all have an experience together as a family. I saw an advertisement for the New Year's Eve train ride in Fort Pike. They have a holiday-themed train ride through the countryside. We can even invite Michael. I think this is something the whole family will enjoy together."

"That's another great idea hon!" Noah said with excitement.

They finally arrived at Walt and Lucille's house in time for the feast. Walt and Lucille lived in a small town in the middle of Tennessee. They parked the car, grabbed Gracelyn's popular cranberry scones, and headed up to the house.

"Let the games begin!" Noah jokingly said to Gracelyn.

Once Thanksgiving occurred, you could practically hear the starting gun as the race to the Christmas chaos began.

Noah and Gracelyn walked up to the door which was covered with classic Tennessee-style wooden black bear statues. Noah knocked on the door and Aunt Lucille answered.

"Oh, come in, come in. I'm so glad you can make it. How was your drive in?" Lucille asked.

"Other than the high speed chase and the two hour traffic jam, it was fine" Noah joked, "No it was actually a nice, pleasant drive in. It gave us time to figure out our Christmas list."

Noah barely made it in the front door and he could not get his jacket off fast enough. A gust of heat overtook him and his forehead immediately began to sweat. Walt and Lillian liked to keep their house temperature at 75 degrees. With the thermostat set so high and with all the guests crammed in there, it was quite toasty inside.

Noah whispered to Gracelyn, "At least I will sweat off all the calories I eat in this sauna."

They made their rounds with all the family members, giving hugs, handshakes, and the yearly family updates. Noah did not mind going since it was family, but after so many years it was starting to feel like the same old thing. It had sort of become a competition between cousins on who had the best vacation that year, who had the most success at work, or what their children had accomplished since they all saw each other last. Noah would play along, but did his best holding back and trying not to get caught up in the bragging contest. He kept reminding himself that it was only for a few hours, to just listen and let them tell their stories, and keep on smiling. It was family and you only see them once a year.

Aunt Lillian finished setting the last casserole on the table and everyone gathered around to pray for their meal. It was a tradition that one of the young children would say the blessing. Gracelyn's cousin, Perry, had a little boy named Jimmy and Aunt Lillian had called on him to do the honors.

Jimmy was six years old and a sharp, quick-witted little boy. You never knew what words would come out of his mouth. Jimmy looked around at everyone to make sure they were ready to pray, he looked up at his dad and Perry gave him the nod to start.

Jimmy bowed his head and prayed, "Dear God, thank you for this food. Thanks for all the hard work Aunt Lillian did. Please don't let my mom make me eat the green bean casserole, and please let there be some pumpkin pie left when I'm ready for dessert. Amen!"

Everyone burst out laughing at Jimmy's prayer.

Perry nodded his head up and down and threw his arms up saying, "Another proud father moment. I have to give Jimmy credit, at least he's honest. Hope you made enough pumpkin pie Aunt Lillian."

When everyone finished the carb overloaded dinner, everyone proceeded to their usually post-

Thanksgiving feast routine. All the men would head to the living room to watch the football game, but most of them barely made it through the first quarter before they fell asleep. The women would clean up all the food and dishes, then huddle around the dining room table to discuss all the Black Friday deals. They would also share their family Christmas gift ideas with each other. The kids would go down to the basement and play ping pong and other games.

Once the first football game was over and the men were done with their naps they would get ready for Uncle Walt's annual basketball tradition. Walt called it the Triple T Classic. The T's stood for: Turkeys, Threes, and Turnovers. This was a tradition Walt started twenty years ago when his oldest son was playing high school basketball and every year, weather permitting, they would play. Most of the men in the family played basketball in their school days and all of them looked forward to this annual event even if there were more turnovers than three pointers made.

Walt was sixty five years old and he was hanging with the best of them. He was probably in the best shape of all of them and he was prepared to show the younger generations that age was just a number.

"You are like a machine, Uncle Walt", Perry said as he was trying to catch his breath.

"Don't underestimate your elders boys", Walt said as he intensely rushed back to get on defense. "Switch to zone defense guys", Walt commanded to his teammates.

Gracelyn had a cousin newly married and her husband, Ryan, was playing basketball with the family for the first time.

Ryan was on offense and he said to Noah, "Man, Uncle Walt is intense."

"He sure is," replied Noah. "He does not like to lose. I think the older he gets the better he gets...and the more competitive he gets," Noah added.

Noah got the ball at the top of the key, swung it around to Perry in the corner, and Perry shot a three pointer. The ball missed and several went for the rebound. One guy peeled off with a cramp and another hobbled away with a pulled hamstring. Uncle Walt was the one who got the rebound, of course. The men finished their game and were exhausted, but with all the energy they burned off they were ready to head back into the house for a second round of Thanksgiving turkey.

Black Friday

About fifteen years ago, after Noah and Gracelyn got married, Noah and his brother started an annual tradition of hitting up Black Friday sales. Michael was a huge fan of technology and he loved getting the best tech bargain he could get. Always having the latest and greatest technology was not kind to Michael's finances and was part of why he struggled financially. When they used to go shopping together, Noah enjoyed the time he spent being with his brother, plus finding a good Christmas gift bargain was an added bonus.

When Noah and his family moved an hour away for his career about eight years ago, it was about the same time that Michael started accelerating his cavalier lifestyle and the brothers' annual Black Friday tradition took a long break. Michael had married a sweetheart of a wife, but his drinking and an affair destroyed his wife's trust in him. After the divorce he accumulated a lot of debt that made it difficult for him.

After several years of a break and rarely seeing each other, Noah decided the break was over. He felt it was time to resurrect the tradition, so he reached out to Michael that Thanksgiving night to persuade him to start the bargain hunting tradition back up again.

When Noah called Michael, it was just at the right time. Michael was pretty down on himself since he had just learned of an upcoming layoff at the coal mine he worked at. This phone call was just what Michael needed and he was excited to start the tradition up again with his little brother. After learning of the layoff, Noah felt in his heart it was his mission to bring their relationship closer together and to help Michael have a special Christmas.

Michael was a firm believer that you had to get to the stores before they opened up. Since Noah lived in a much bigger city than Michael, there were many more shopping choices for them. Michael had picked up a second job driving a parts delivery van in the evening for a computer parts distributor, so he could not drive into Noah's the night before.

The game plan was for Michael to meet at Noah's house at 5:30 a.m. Noah thought it was a little nuts to start that early, especially when it was still dark out. Noah and his family had the four hour round trip the day before to Uncle Walt and Aunt Lillian's and he would have loved to sleep in a little more that morning. However, in order to save that money and be with his brother it meant he had to get up at 5:00 a.m. to get ready in time.

Michael rolled up in front of Noah's house at 5:30 a.m. on the dot. Noah was stunned because his brother was late for everything in life. For some reason, Black Friday was the one day of the year that Michael decided he would be punctual. Noah got in the car and was surprised to see an assortment of beverages greeting him. There were drinks in the console, on the floor board, on the dash, and even in the passenger seat. Michael had just about every drink choice Noah could choose from. There were three brands of energy drinks, orange juice, several brands of caffeinated soft drinks, and Michael even made a stop to get Noah a hot cup of coffee.

"Take your pick", said Michael.

"Thanks, Michael," Noah replied as he was moving drinks around in order to get seated properly.

"How much do I owe you?" Noah asked.

"Ah, it's nothing. Consider it my treat for you taking time away from your family today and being thoughtful enough to help restart our old deal finding tradition," Michael gladly replied.

Noah looked through all the drinks and picked the coffee. Not realizing Noah was starting to take a sip, Michael floored it, and coffee spilled on Noah's face and shirt.

"Oops. Sorry about that," Michael said apologetically, "I'm just excited for the deal finding duo to take off and get there early."

"You can slow it down a little bit Speedy. We're not going to fight crime sidekick." Noah half-jokingly replied.

"Sidekick?" Michael asked.

"Well you did call us a deal finding duo," Noah laughed, "Is that "S" on your shirt for savings?"

"So I can tell this is going to be a fun-filled day of zingers. Be ready Captain Funny Man,"

Michael said as he proceeded on driving to the first store.

The first stop was the Electronic Gadgets & Gizmos store. They were giving the first hundred customers a $50 gift card and their biggest sale item was a 50" LED 4K television for only $300. Michael really wanted to get this television. His television at home was about ten years old and had lines in it which distorted the picture. He knew that this was an unbelievable deal that he could not pass it up.

When they got to the store it was just getting ready to open up. There were close to a hundred people already standing in front of the store. A few people at the front of the line even had a tent up, so they must have camped out all night just to get the gift card or some other deal.

Shaking his head in disbelief, Noah said, "I can't believe this. It's freezing out here and all these people are already lined up."

Michael laughed and said, "Deals brother, it's for the deals."

They parked the car and headed over to the back of the line. The temperature was freezing and Noah had thoughts of regret for being the one to start this tradition back up.

With teeth chattering, Noah mumbled, "I can't believe we are doing this. The deals will probably be better on Cyber Monday."

"That's possible," Michael replied, "but this is all part of taking in the experience with your big brother. Plus it is our old tradition."

"You are right. I'm sorry I questioned our being here," replied Noah as he stood there chattering his teeth, "We'll have a good time, I know."

The doors opened at 6:00 a.m. and it was a free for all. As they approached the employee passing out the gift cards, the lady in front of them got the very last one. Hoping this was not going to be a sign for how the day would go, they darted over to the television section. Michael was hopeful that the television he was looking for was still available. Apparently everyone in front of them was after the same deal.

As they got closer you could hear yelling, and a couple security guards rushed over to the section. The section was jam packed full of carts and people. Michael's confidence level in getting the television was diminishing. People started walking away slowly, and the brothers knew this was not promising. Customers were grumbling and upset since the televisions were all gone.

"Well I guess that's my luck," Michael said as he was disappointed about the televisions being sold out.

"Sorry about that," Noah replied, "Maybe we will come across some other good sales." "Possibly, but this was the number one thing I wanted to get today. My television is a piece of trash and I don't have the money to buy a nice one like this at normal price," Michael explained as his mood totally changed.

Trying to lift his spirits, Noah said, "Let's get out of here and march on to the other stores. There are deals to be found and I'm confident that our luck will pick up again."

Noah and Michael shopped all day long. They bounced around from store to store. They read every sales insert and went to what felt like a hundred stores looking for a deal they could not pass up.

At a little past 5:00 p.m., Michael finally threw in the towel, "Look, I'm having fun shopping with you and we've had some minor success in finding a few nice deals, but I'm finished. The early morning is catching up with me and I am done with these crowds.

Relieved by Michael's decision, Noah said, "I'm with you big brother. It has been fun, and you're right we did score a few bargains. Let's head back to my house and have dinner. Gracelyn was planning on making her famous chicken parmesan tonight. I think that used to be a favorite of yours."

"Now we are talking. Let's high tail it out of here," Michael said in a cheerfully excited tone. Both of the guys proceeded to get in the car.

Right before Noah started to take a sip of his drink he looked over at Michael and said, "I know you are excited for chicken parmesan, but before you gun it Speedy, let me take a swig of this before I add cola to the coffee on my shirt."

Michael laughed and gave Noah time to settle into his seat and take a drink before he headed back to Noah's house.

The guys got back to Noah's house and Gracelyn was preparing dinner for the family.

"Smells good Gracelyn!" Michael said.

"Oh, hi Michael. I made extra, so you can take some home with you for the weekend," Gracelyn said.

Grinning ear to ear, Michael replied, "That's awesome! Did I ever tell you that you were my favorite sister-in-law?"

"I'm your only sister-in-law Michael," Gracelyn said as she rolled her eyes.

As they sat at the dining room table and started to eat, Michael asked Gracelyn, "So, do you guys still put up your Christmas decorations during Thanksgiving weekend?"

Practically jumping up and down, Gracelyn replied, "Yes, Yes, Yes! I can't wait. Noah will get all the decorations out of the attic tomorrow morning and then we spend most of Saturday decorating."

"Do you guys still have the wooden Santa and reindeer decorations you place outside?" Michael asked.

Gracelyn replied, "We still put them out each year. They are starting to show their age, but from a distance they still look great. We still need a good nativity set though. We've tried the plastic figures, but they look too cheap and cheesy. By the time I get around to thinking about ordering a wooden set, it's too late. The guys that make those need your order in August, and who remembers to do that during that time of the year? They are a little pricey too. Who knows, maybe someday we can get a nice set to display out there. That's really the last missing piece of all our indoor and outdoor decorations."

"So, Liam, what's on your Christmas list this year?" Michael asked Noah's son.

Excited to tell his uncle what he wanted for Christmas, Liam said, "I want the C.H.A.M.P. Robot. So does Emma."

"Yes, definitely that robot," Emma added, "It's super cool! It plays games with you, plays music, and it can even help me with some of my school work."

"Well for educational reasons alone, this sounds like the perfect toy for Christmas," Michael replied.

"It is pretty expensive and very hard to find. Plus, we still have a month of good behavior needed before there's a chance that Santa could get it," Noah replied as he was relieved to hear his idea matched his kids' idea.

Quick to reply, Liam told his dad, "Dad, Santa can make anything. That's all we really want anyways, so trust me we will be on our best behavior. Right Emma?"

"Yes, Liam," Emma reluctantly agreed.

"Before you leave Michael, I've got this picture matte I want us to all put our handprints on. It's going to go around a collage of photographs of you and I as kids, plus our family with the kiddos. I figured mom and dad would like to put this up in their house," Noah said to Michael.

They finished their dinner and continued catching up with each over during the course of the evening. Gracelyn hoped this was the start of a closer relationship between the two brothers.

She knew it was important to Noah and she felt she was witnessing the strengthening of their brotherly bond.

The Joyful Drummer

The Monday after Thanksgiving break, Noah was outside his office building heading into work. Before he rounded the corner to the lobby door, he heard a very entertaining drum beat in the background. He glanced to his left and noticed a group of people smiling and dancing as they stood around a street musician. Noah could not see the person from where he stood, so he crossed over the street to see the performer up close.

Performing for the crowd was a man in his late forties playing drums on a variety of empty plastic buckets, wooden crates, and a drum. The gentleman also had some type of makeshift cymbal device as well. In front of this unique drum set was an empty jar with a sign that read: "If my music put a smile on your face, I would be honored if you donated." Impressed by the sound, Noah felt a tug on his heart.

After years of ignoring these type of donation requests on the streets, he decided to give the man ten dollars. As he was leaning down to give the man the money, he noticed a C.I.S.U. wrestling sticker on a bucket. The man finished up his song, thanked the crowd, and grabbed his bottled water for a quick break.

Trying to catch the man in between sets, Noah asked, "I see your C.I.S.U. wrestling sticker on your bucket there. Did you wrestle for them?"

Startled at first that someone actually spoke to him, the man said, "Oh, uh yes. I sure did. I wrestled there and actually was a wrestling referee back in the day."

Noah never gave money to people on the street, let alone talk to them. Call it a prompting from God, call it what you want, but he felt called to help the guy out and just have a conversation with the man. Sure it was cold outside, and he had a meeting he needed to get to, but he felt like he could do a little more for this man than just give him some money. Noah did wonder what the man would use the money for, but who was he to judge he thought to himself. When he felt that prompting he knew he had to act on it and give the joyful performer a donation.

The man on the street thanked Noah several times. "Thank you so much. God bless you, sir.

This is very generous of you and this will really help me," the man said.

"You're welcome. You earned it," Noah replied and then he reluctantly asked, "I hope you have a warm place to retreat to out of this cold?"

"Yes I do. Thank you for asking. I'm not homeless. I have an apartment where my family and I live. I love bringing joy to people and playing music allows me to do just that. I can use a talent God gave me and it's an honest living. I feel better doing this instead of asking for a handout. This allows me to give a little something back," the man said.

Pointing at the wrestling sticker with his drum stick the man asked Noah, "So, do you know much about wrestling?"

"I know a little. My best friend in high school wrestled. I tried it my sophomore year after he asked me to try it, but I broke my wrist in the second practice. Needless to say that was the end of my wrestling career," Noah replied.

The man laughed and said, "I'm sorry to hear you didn't have a better experience. Wrestling is a great sport. It takes a lot of discipline and is demanding, but it is very rewarding. You better get to work and so should I. Thank you again and I hope you have a blessed Christmas. I'm Sam by the way," the man told Noah as he reached over to shake his hand.

Feeling like he just made a new friend, Noah shook his hand and said, "Nice to meet you Sam. I'm Noah. It was a pleasure talking with you and thanks for putting me in a cheerful mood before I head to work."

Sam smiled and continued to create more joy with his drums for all the people passing by.

Spiritually Fed

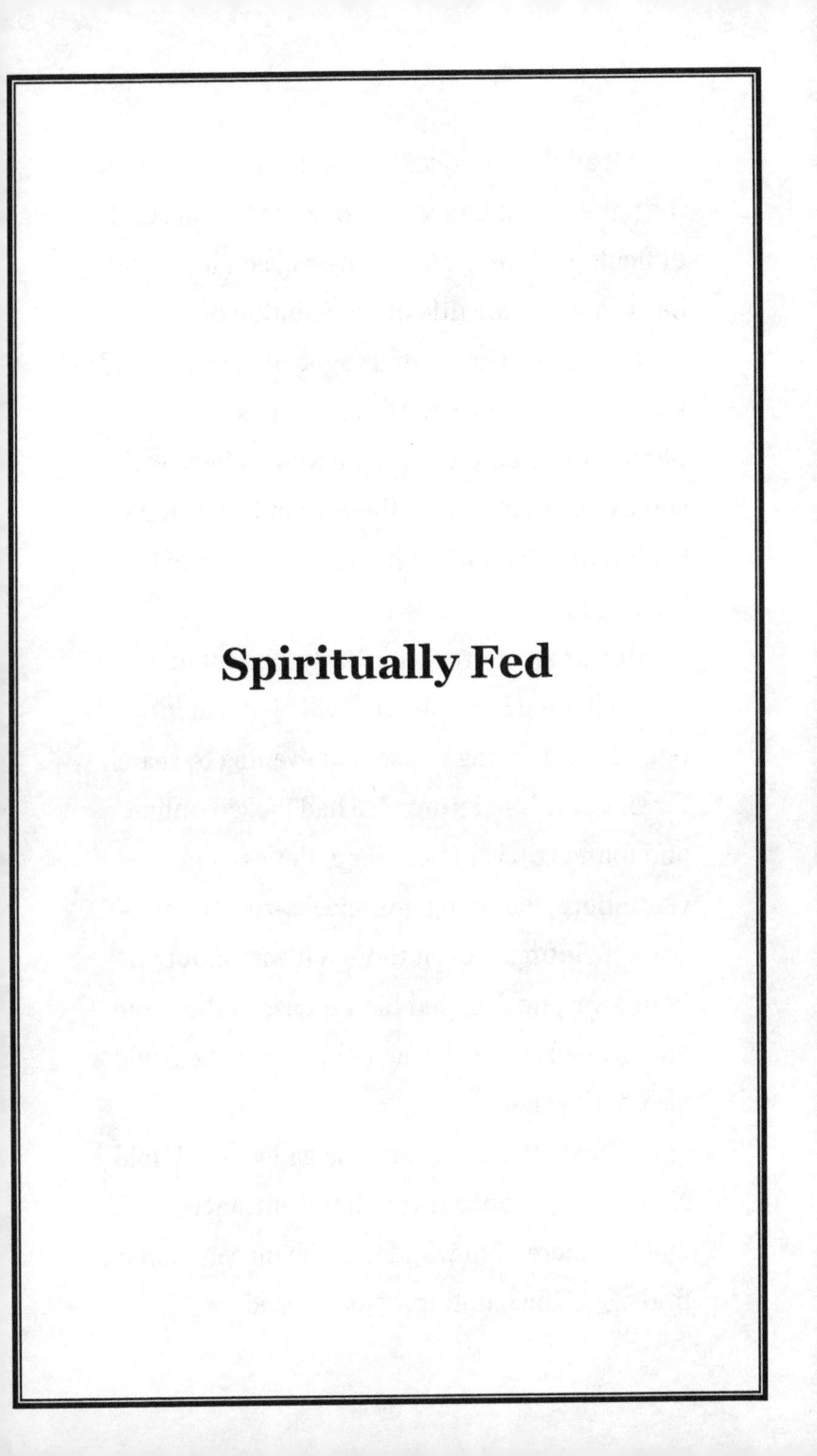

Of all the gift ideas he had to get, Noah knew the painting for Gracelyn would be the most difficult to obtain. He had never seen it nor did he even know the title of the painting or the artist's name. Going off a vague description and knowing Gracelyn saw it in the Smoky Mountains, Noah thought he would check with some of the galleries in the Pigeon Forge and Gatlinburg areas while he was in Knoxville for a business trip.

It was an afternoon in early December and Noah checked in to his Knoxville hotel at 3:00 p.m. He was going to use that evening to search for Gracelyn's painting. He had looked online and found two very popular galleries in Gatlinburg, including one specializing in faith-based paintings. Even though it was about an hour away, he dropped his suitcase in the room and headed straight back to his car, so he could visit both galleries.

"Good afternoon, sir," the gallery clerk told Noah as he stepped through the entrance.

"Hi there. I'm wondering if you can help me find a specific painting," Noah asked.

"I'll do my best to help. Do you know the title or the artist?" the clerk replied.

"No, just a vague description my wife gave me. It's from several years ago. She said it was a traditional style church that you could see inside of, there were wooden pews and stained glass windows all around, a person praying, and it had a bald eagle rising out above it. Does that description sound familiar by chance?" Noah asked with little hope.

Shaking her head no, the clerk said, "No, can't say I've ever seen a painting like that. Let me check with Frank in the back. He's the owner and has been here for 48 years. He moves a little slow, but he's got the best memory of anyone I know."

The clerk went to the back office and out came an elderly man with a walker.

"She says you need some help finding a painting?" Frank asked.

Hoping Frank could help, Noah said, "I sure do. I'm in Knoxville for business and I'm trying to surprise my wife for Christmas with this painting she saw in this neck of the woods years ago. It's a traditional looking church, with wooden pews, stained glass windows, and a bald eagle that is coming out of the top of it. Have any idea where I could find it?"

Frank looked behind the desk, staring at the wall with a grin. "Mister. Believe it or not, I do. It used to be here for a long time and now I see it every Sunday. I see it in the fellowship hall of our church every Sunday," Frank replied.

"That's great. I'm glad to hear you know where it's at. Would you by chance know if the church would be willing to sell it?" Noah asked.

"I'm not sure if they would, but let me give you the address of the church and you can go find out. The pastor should be there since they are preparing the food pantry donations for tonight," Frank replied.

Pumped up with excitement, Noah drove to the Salvation in the Smoky Mountains Chapel. At first impression Noah was surprised to know a church this small could survive and still be operating. It was a small mountainside chapel that looked like it was out of a painting itself. The chapel was surrounded by towering trees and a tranquil sounding creek flowed along the side of the church.

Noah headed up to the sanctuary entrance and walked in since the door was open. Greeted by a man walking by with a box of canned goods, "Hello there. I'm Pastor Mark. Are you here to help setup for the food pantry tonight?"

"Oh no, sorry," replied Noah, "I'm Noah and Frank at the art gallery said you might be able to help me out."

"Do you need prayer?" Pastor Mark asked.

"I'm sure I could use some, but I'm actually here about a painting. There's a painting I'm looking for as a gift for my wife. She saw it years ago while on vacation with her parents and she always wished she had bought it. I figured this Christmas I would try to hunt it down and surprise her with it, if the price was right," Noah laughed.

Pastor Mark was intrigued by Noah's request. Curious to learn more about the painting this new visitor was looking for he said, "Follow me back to the fellowship hall, so I can drop off this box of food and we'll see if I can help you out. I'm not sure we have what you are looking for and even if we did, it's probably not something we could sell."

Noah and Pastor Mark made their way back to the fellowship hall and Noah looked up and down the walls. There were paintings of Jesus and The Last Supper, photographs of the congregation at different events, mission trip photos, and in the corner stood an American flag which beside it was the painting Gracelyn desired.

"There it is!" Noah pointed to the painting, "That's got to be what Gracelyn wanted."

Both of them walked over to the painting and Pastor Mark said, "If you have a few minutes, let me tell you the story about this painting."

Eager to learn more, Noah agreed with Pastor Mark, "Yes, please tell me all about it."

"Great," said Pastor Mark and he continued to share the amazing story.

"Several years ago it used to be up in the gallery you visited. There was only this original and no copies were ever made. A family who used to go to church here, before they moved away, had purchased it for their son. Their son was a true patriot. He joined the military after the tragedy of 9/11 and fought in the Iraq War. He was very active in our youth ministry. He loved Jesus and he loved his country. He even had an eagle tattoo on his arm. His parents bought this painting as a gift for him when he would return from the war, but sadly enough he never returned. They donated it to the church before they moved and we've had it up here beside the flag and his picture ever since."

Noah looked on the other side of the flag and there was a picture of the courageous young man in his military uniform.

Saddened by the story, Noah said, "Wow, I don't know what to say. Words can't describe how this painting makes you feel. I am amazed by it. Even before you told me that story, I could see why my wife fell in love with it years ago. It is truly a moving piece of art. I wish the solider would have been able to see it. Thank you for telling me the story. This painting clearly belongs here and I definitely have to bring my wife here to see it again in person. Do you mind if I take a picture of it?"

The pastor nodded yes and backed away, so Noah could proceed with taking a picture of the painting along with the soldier's picture.

"You are welcome to visit us anytime," the pastor told Noah as he patted him on the shoulder, "Actually we are having a small volunteer dinner here in twenty minutes before we open up the food pantry. I'd be honored if you stayed and joined us. The Miller sisters always cook up way more than we can eat."

Looking at his watch and knowing he did not have any dinner plans, Noah agreed. The two continued moving some food boxes in to the pantry until everyone else arrived.

"I would like to thank everyone for being here tonight," Pastor Mark said, "We could not serve the community like this if it weren't for dedicated volunteers like you all. I would like to thank the Miller sisters for their gracious hearts and providing us some fabulous food to eat before we serve. I would also like to introduce to you our visiting friend, Noah. Let's all go to the

Lord in prayer. Dear Heavenly Father, we would like to thank you for giving us this opportunity to serve you and others. Thank you for all these amazing volunteers and the hard work they have put into this. We thank you for this food and ask that you will bless this food and bless this evening. We ask that you will use us to help these people and give us opportunities to bring them closer to you. We say these things in the name of Jesus Christ. Amen."

While eating their meal one of the church elders sitting across from Noah asked him, "So, where are you on your spiritual journey?"

Stumbling his words at first since he was surprised by the question, Noah replied, "Uh....well....I'm not exactly sure, but I do know I have a lot of room to grow spiritually."

"We all do, brother," he joked back, "Do you attend church regularly?"

"No I don't," Noah embarrassingly replied, "I am a believer in God, in Jesus, but with work and family I don't make my faith a priority. We make sure we go at Easter and Christmas, but outside of that our involvement in church is pretty sparse."

"You know what you are? You are a Chreaster." the elder said.

"A what?" asked Noah.

"A Chreaster. That's what I call folks who only attend on Christmas and Easter. Don't worry, we'll get you set straight before you leave," he laughed.

After everyone finished eating, they all sprung up and assembled into their assigned stations in the Food Pantry. Noah could not help but feel a prompting in his heart that was telling him to stay and help serve. He had no other plans, it was still early in the evening, and he was just going to go back to the hotel and work. He had never served like this before, but he knew it was the right thing to do.

Going over to the pastor, Noah asked, "Pastor Mark, I appreciate your kindness this evening and since I don't have any other plans, I would love to help out if you could use me."

"That's wonderful," said the pastor, "We can sure use your help. We'll have you be a shopper and all you do is walk with the person and help them get the things on the checklist. It's so much fun and very rewarding." "Let's open the doors folks and share the Good News of Jesus!" Pastor Mark shouted with excitement.

The next two hours changed Noah's life. He heard all kinds of stories from people who were out of a job, a couple having financial struggles, single parents, and more stories that touched his heart. He realized that all the work and money he and his family spent on Christmas gifts was quite silly. He was serving people that needed help just getting food to eat, something that had never been an issue for him. Christmas gifts were the least of these people's worries.

As Noah helped people out that night he noticed volunteers praying with the guests, and he also noticed a flyer that went in each box that the people received. Curious of what the letter said, he took one out to read it. It was about the meaning of Christmas and had an invitation to visit a service at the chapel.

That evening was a turning point for Noah. He was starting to think about Christmas in a different, more appreciative way. He knew that moving forward he needed to use his resources more effectively. Just like Sam used his gift of playing the drums to bring joy to others, Noah decided he needed to allocate more of his time and money each month to help others.

When the last guest left, everyone started cleaning up. Pastor Mark came over to Noah and asked him what he thought about his serving experience.

"That was amazing Mark," Noah ecstatically said, "I'm so glad I did this."

Pastor Mark looked at Noah and said, "I bet you did not think this evening you would be fed dinner, help feed others, and be spiritually fed somehow did you?"

Noah smiled and told the pastor, "This night helped me see things in a totally different light. Thank you for allowing me to be a part of it."

Wild Goose Chase

When Noah decided to get Emma and Liam the C.H.A.M.P. Robot for Christmas, he thought, "How hard could it be with almost three weeks to go until Christmas?" He totally underestimated the popularity and availability of this little robotic phenomenon. Emma even told her dad that she thought it was unrealistic to get since she knew they were hard to find. Liam on the other hand, thought "Santa could make anything," so that put more pressure on Noah to get it. Noah could not let "Santa" disappoint Liam.

"Christmas list? Check. Wallet? Check. Car Keys? Check. Phone? Check," Noah said to himself as he prepared to venture out into the shopping pandemonium. This Christmas season Noah would take a vacation day from work to go shopping. His objective was to knock out a majority of his and Gracelyn's Christmas list, especially items he knew he could not find online or wanted to see in person before he purchased. Number one on the list was the C.H.A.M.P. Robot. Since the toy was exclusive at Toy Fortress he assumed he would not have much trouble since there were four stores around the city.

Arriving at the Toy Fortress closest to their home, Noah could not believe his eyes. The parking lot was swarming with cars and people. Cars were honking and he was already feeling his stress levels peak. After ten minutes of driving around, Noah finally found a parking spot on the back side of the store. When he got in the store, he immediately tracked down a clerk to help him.

"Excuse me, could you help me find something?" Noah asked.

"Let me guess, you're looking for the C.H.A.M.P. Robot?" the clerk sarcastically responded.

"I am. Do you have it?" Noah replied.

"We did, about two weeks ago. There's no guarantee if we'll get any more in before Christmas either," the clerk replied in an exhaustive tone.

"Could you check another store for me?" Noah asked.

"I guess. Let me get to a computer," the clerk said as he threw the toys he was stocking on the shelves back into the cart and stormed off to the computer.

"Ok, call it your lucky day, but the Westgate location shows they have one in stock. Someone may have returned it or it got lost in the warehouse. Better hurry up or it will be gone any second," the clerk told Noah.

Noah thanked the clerk and dashed out the store to drive to the Westgate Toy Fortress.

Approaching the second store, Noah noticed it was not as busy as the previous store. He was feeling good about this store having the robot.

Noah went into the store and quickly rushed to a clerk to ask, "I was just at another location, and they said you have one C.H.A.M.P. Robot left. Can you show me where it is?"

"Sir, I don't think we have any left. I haven't seen one for a few days. Let's go take a look," the clerk said as they headed through the store.

When they got to the section the robot had been displayed at it was empty.

"Sorry sir, just like I thought, we don't have any left," the clerk said to Noah.

"But the other store said you had one left," Noah said with disappointment.

Feeling bad for Noah, the clerk said, "I'm so sorry sir. We've been so busy here and it's been extremely difficult to keep our inventories accurate. It's best to call us before you come so we can make sure the item is available and we can put it on hold for you."

"I should have called before I wasted my time driving twenty miles to get here. Thanks anyway for your help. Could you check one of the other two locations?" Noah asked.

Both of them headed up to the customer service desk and Noah's hope grew once more. The clerk called the store in Piermont and they said they just found one that got lost in their warehouse. Noah graciously thanked the clerk and hurried off to get to Piermont so he could mark the robot off his list of things to get today.

"Third time's a charm," Noah said to himself out loud as he walked into the Piermont Toy Fortress store. He headed over to the customer service desk and asked for the robot they had put on hold.

"Here you go mister. You sure got lucky with us finding this back in the warehouse. It's a little banged up, but it's never been opened," the clerk said to Noah.

Looking at the box in shocking disappointment, "Are you kidding me?" Noah said, "The box looks like it's been through a game of shopping cart basketball. How can I give this as a gift?"

Getting very nervous as he could sense Noah ready to explode at any moment, the clerk said, "I'm so sorry. I'm really, really sorry. I can understand your point. It's the last one we have. I can give you a 20% discount if that would help."

Fuming, Noah leaned over to the clerk, looked him in the eyes, and said, "My son thinks Santa's going to get him this. Do you think it looks good that the most expensive gift under the Christmas tree, from Santa, looks like a toy that's been used? I don't think so." Noah gave the box back to the clerk and stormed out the store.

As Noah was getting ready to get in his car, he heard someone trying to get his attention. "Sir, sir, excuse me sir," a festive looking and jolly man in his sixties said as he approached Noah, "I couldn't help but over hear your dilemma. There is the Toy Box store up in Maplewood that might have what you are looking for. They specialize in unique and hard to find toys. Give them a try."

Frustrated with the wild goose chase that had consumed most of his morning, Noah replied, "Thanks. This will probably be my last effort before I have to move on to another Christmas idea for the kids. Thanks for the helpful info. I appreciate that!"

Noah typed the store into his phone's map app and away he went. The Toy Box was in a rough part of the city, but at this point he was willing to go there if it could gain him the robot.

He arrived in Maplewood and on the main street he saw a little store called, "The Toy Box". It was not busy like the other toy stores and he just assumed they did not offer much.

He walked into the store and as his eyes got bigger he said to himself, "Wow. I can't believe all these toys I've never seen before."

He looked at the price tags and quickly realized why the store was not very busy.

Everything was two to three times higher than the normal retail price.

He went to the checkout desk and the store owner hung up the phone. "What brings you to the Toy Box?" the owner asked.

"I'm looking for the C.H.A.M.P. Robot. Do you have one?" Noah replied.

"As a matter of fact I do. It's on an online auction right now, but for the right price I may be able to close the auction early and sell it to you," the owner said with a grin.

"I've been all over God's green Earth, so I'm willing to pay a premium...within reason," Noah told him in an irritated tone.

The owner went back to his office and brought his laptop out to show Noah the current bid price of the robot. "It's fetching $475 right now and I've still got two days to go," the owner said.

"How about $500?" Noah asked.

"No way dude. Two days from now the highest bidder will be closer to $800," the owner arrogantly said.

"Look, I'm willing to pay you $700 for it today. There is no guarantee you will get more than that on your auction and you don't have to mess with shipping it. I have got $200 on me now and I will go get the rest at the bank. $700 cash?" begged Noah.

"Alright, in the spirit of Christmas, I'll help you out. $700 it is."

Noah shook hands with the owner and hurried off to get the rest of the money.

After he purchased the robot, he called Gracelyn, "Spirit of Christmas. Ha! This toy store made several hundred dollars off me. Supply and demand, I guess. Oh well. I have not had much luck today, but I will see you at dinner."

Homerun Surprise

Noah knew that while he did not know exactly what the gift would be for his boss, he knew that the path he was going down by trying to get something baseball related from his alma mater would be a grand slam of an idea. Noah's boss held their department Christmas party the week before Christmas. With a shorter lead time to get the gift, he knew he would have to start immediately.

It was a Wednesday, two weeks prior to the party, and Noah decided to make some inquiries at Kingstown State University during lunch. Noah closed his office door and called the athletic department at the school. When he described that he was trying to locate any type of baseball memorabilia during his boss's career there, they lead him straight to Barney the long time field manager.

Barney was an old-fashioned guy in his early seventies. Unfortunately, for Noah, Barney did not have a phone since he was more of a meet face-to-face kind of guy. Determined to get his boss something from there, he decided to take the rest of the day off to drive there and meet Barney.

"Hey hon," Noah said to Gracelyn over the phone as he walked to his car, "I'm taking the afternoon off and heading to Kingstown State. I'm going to see if the baseball field manager can help me out on Hank's gift."

He finished up the call and set out on his journey to Kingstown State. The university was located about 45 miles away, but that was not going to stop Noah from trying to get a unique gift.

One hour later, Noah arrived at the baseball field. Being the winter, the season was over, but from what the athletic department said, Barney was the type of guy always at the field. It was his sanctuary and he was always making improvements there. Noah walked around the outside of the field and did not see anyone. Then he heard some hammering in the visitor's dugout. He walked over to the dugout and there was a man just like the athletic department described.

"Barney?" Noah said to the gentleman.

"The one and only. How may I be of service to you?" Barney replied.

Excited to know he found Barney, Noah proceeded with telling him about his gift goal, "Hi, I'm Noah and I'm hoping you could help me out with a gift idea. When I called the athletic department they said you were the perfect man to talk to since you knew a lot about the baseball history here and you may actually have some memorabilia collected from over the years. See, I'm trying to find a unique gift for my boss for Christmas. He played baseball here in the late '80's and from what I understand he was a pretty good catcher. His name is Hank Newsome. Do you remember him?"

Nodding his head up and down, Barney replied, "I sure do. Pretty good catcher you say? He was an excellent catcher! In all my years here, I have never seen a catcher pop up and thrown down to second base so fast and so accurately. Let's go in the building where it's warmer."

The two continued their talks in the field equipment building. Barney loved to talk baseball and you could tell he had a true passion for the game. They talked about baseball for over an hour while Barney looked through boxes, pausing often to share a baseball story. Noah learned more about various baseball legends then he ever thought he would. With the crash course in baseball legend history he just received he was ready to go on a sports trivia game show.

"Here, help me get this box down," Barney said to Noah.

It was a heavy box and it had a piece of masking tape for a label with the handwritten words on it saying, "Bases Pre 1990". Barney took the lid off the box and started pulling out bases. Then he pulled out a home plate.

"Many players have taken an at bat by this plate, many have touched this plate to score a run, and some of those guys went on to play in the big leagues. This home plate was used for many years before we purchased all new bases in 1990. Your boss, Hank, caught right behind this," Barney proudly said.

It was like Barney had discovered some long lost treasure and Noah could not believe his eyes.

"That is so cool. I can't believe you would still have something like this. I expected maybe an old game program at best, but to have the actual plate he caught behind and batted at...that's truly remarkable," Noah said in awe.

"You know, many people these days don't appreciate the history of baseball. I know Hank would appreciate something like this and I appreciate you even thinking of doing something like this. A gift like this keeps the history alive. Here you go. I know he'll enjoy it," Barney said as he handed the base to Noah.

"I think he'll enjoy it too. He will be stunned to see this. I know he'll be grateful to both of us for giving it to him. Thank you so much," Noah said as he shook Barney's hand.

Noah left Kingstown State feeling like he had just won the lottery. He was so thankful for what Barney gave him and he knew his boss, Hank, would be so happy with this special gift. Noah wanted to put the home plate in a frame so Hank could properly display it, so he reached out to his brother, Michael, to see if he could put his woodworking skills to work.

"Is this the number one carpenter in the state?" Noah asked Michael over the phone. Michael replied,

"Well I'm no Jesus, but I've done some woodworking in the past."

"I need your help and it can earn you some extra cash for the holidays," Noah offered, "It's a long story, but basically I have a baseball home plate I want to get framed. It's a Christmas gift for my boss."

"Sure, I'd be happy to do it and you know me....I could use some extra cash right now. Just bring it on by," Michael said.

Noah got off the phone and during his drive to Michael's house he started thinking of gift ideas he could get his brother this Christmas.

It was about 8 p.m. in the evening and Noah pulled up in front of Michael's house. He was outside smoking with another guy. Noah had never seen this person before, so he just assumed it was a friend or neighbor.

As soon as Noah parked, the other guy hurried into the garage and closed the door while Michael stayed outside. It looked very suspicious and Noah had a real bad feeling that they were not up to any good. Noah knew Michael's past too well and he could not help but think that Michael may have been dabbling in trouble with all the issues he had been going through.

Disappointed in what he was assuming, Noah got out of the car and handed Michael the home plate.

"Hey. I did not mean to interrupt your company," Noah said.

"Oh, that's fine. We were just hanging out. He just closed the garage door because it's cold and the garage is a mess," Michael replied.

Noah did not quite believe his brother, but he did not say anything. He was exhausted from the busy day and was ready to get back home to see his family.

A Surprise Encounter

As he marked another day off his calendar, Noah was looking forward to his upcoming Christmas vacation. It was the day of the office Christmas party and also when they usually received their Christmas bonus. For the past six years, he had received a $500 bonus. Noah knew that was pretty generous in today's corporate environment which rarely gave employees a Christmas bonus anymore.

He could not wait to give his boss, Hank, the home plate he had Michael frame for him. Michael dropped off the frame that morning at the front desk in a giant Christmas bag for Noah. Noah pulled it out of the bag and said to himself, "Michael did a really good job on this," and he proceeded to put the frame behind his desk. Since it was a gift just from him, his plan was to give Hank his gift right after they returned from lunch.

Noah had a morning full of meetings and problems. It was typical at the end of the year and all the office drama was weighing down his Christmas spirit. He was starting to get this overwhelming feeling because he still had things to get before Christmas, and finish the surprise for Gracelyn. The challenge of time was compounding the pressure and he still had so much to do at work if he was going to be able to take any vacation time to spend with his family.

It was lunch time and while his work load was demanding his time, Noah knew he needed to step out for the party. "Come on Noah. It's party time!" a colleague shouted outside his doorway. Noah got out of his chair and joined his colleagues as they headed to the restaurant. He had never eaten there before and just expected the experience and the party to be the same as past years. However, this lunch would change his life.

As everyone ate their lunch and shared stories, Noah was still stressed out with all the work ahead of him. He kept getting calls from the office, which was distracting him even more from enjoying the party. He was never good at disconnecting from work in a social setting, or even when he got home. Noah got another call from work and decided to step away where it was quieter so he could hear the person better. As he stepped away, he heard someone come in the front door singing Christmas music. He turned around and it was Sam the street performing drummer whom he had met a few weeks prior.

"Hey Noah!" Sam softly said to Noah while trying not to disturb his call.

Noah finished his call and greeted Sam, "Hi Sam. How's it going?"

"It's a blessed day," Sam replied, "The sun is shining, Christmas is almost here, and I'm getting ready to work."

"Do you work here?" asked Noah.

"Yep, I'm a cook here," said Sam, "You probably thought all I did was drum all day on the streets," Sam laughed.

"Uh, well...." Noah said as he mumbled his words.

"That's ok. I do both. I work five, sometimes six days a week here. I'll even be here Christmas eve. This is a good steady job and in my free time I entertain on the streets. Like I told you when I met you, it allows me to bring joy to others, plus I make a little more money for my family," Sam proudly said.

The humble Sam shifted his focus over to Noah and asked, "I couldn't help notice you look like you're stressed out about something. What's bugging you?"

"I am a little stressed out. There is so much to do in such little time, tons of stress at work right now, a bunch of things to buy and do before Christmas, and this is our Christmas party which I'm not able to really enjoy right now because my mind is back in the office," Noah said in a frustrated voice.

Feeling sorry for Noah, Sam put his arm on his shoulder, "Noah, that's the problem with Christmas time. Everyone lets all these things stress them out, when it's really a time of celebration. Sure you can get stressed out, but it's all about putting everything in perspective."

"Each time I have seen you, you are so happy. So, what is your trick for putting things in perspective?" asked Noah.

Sam welcomed the question giving him an opportunity to share his approach.

"For me, part of putting things in perspective is about having contentment," Sam told Noah,

"It's not about owning expensive things or having a fancy job title. It's about being happy with what you have and what you do. Sure, I work two jobs, but I enjoy them. They reward me in ways more than what my paycheck reflects. It's what we do in the roles that we have."

Continuing to share his perspective, Sam enlightened Noah by saying, "The other part of how I gain my perspective, is knowing that we have a God who loves us so much. Christmas is about the birth of our Lord and Savior, Jesus Christ. That's what we are celebrating. When we admit we are sinners and ask for forgiveness, when we believe that Jesus died for our sins and rose from the dead, and when we choose to place our faith and trust in Jesus Christ and decide to follow Him, then we are saved by His grace and can have an eternal life in Heaven. It's really that simple. Noah, there is so much for us to be thankful for. Be thankful for what you have, be thankful for your job, be thankful for your family, and be thankful for Jesus. We can't let all these little trivial stresses in life bring our spirits down. That my friend is how I put it all in perspective."

Noah reflected on Sam's words as he returned to the party. His mood totally changed and it was what he needed to hear. The party finished up and everyone started to head back to the office. Noah did not finish all of his meal, so the waitress boxed it up for him. As he put it in the break room refrigerator he noticed there was another small box. It had a note that had the word "Perspective" written on it and a smiley face below it. Noah opened up the box and inside was a piece of homemade apple pie that Sam had given him.

When he got back to his desk, Noah grabbed the framed home plate and headed to Hank's office.

"Thanks for lunch and the Christmas bonus, Hank," Noah said.

"You are very welcome. You earned it," replied Hank.

"Here's something I hope you like. Merry Christmas," said Noah as he handed Hank the gift.

Hank pulled the frame out of the bag and had a puzzled look on his face. "A baseball home plate," Hank said and then he read the label, "Kingstown State University Knights Baseball – Game Used Home Plate 1980-1989."

"That was the home plate you caught behind during the time you played there. I actually got it from Barney the Field Manager there," Noah happily replied.

Shocked by Noah's thoughtfulness, Hank said, "This is the most thoughtful gift anyone has ever given me. Thank you so much!"

Noah headed back to his office, but with the pep talk Sam gave him and the gift success for his boss, he was ready to tackle his afternoon with the new perspective he learned at lunch.

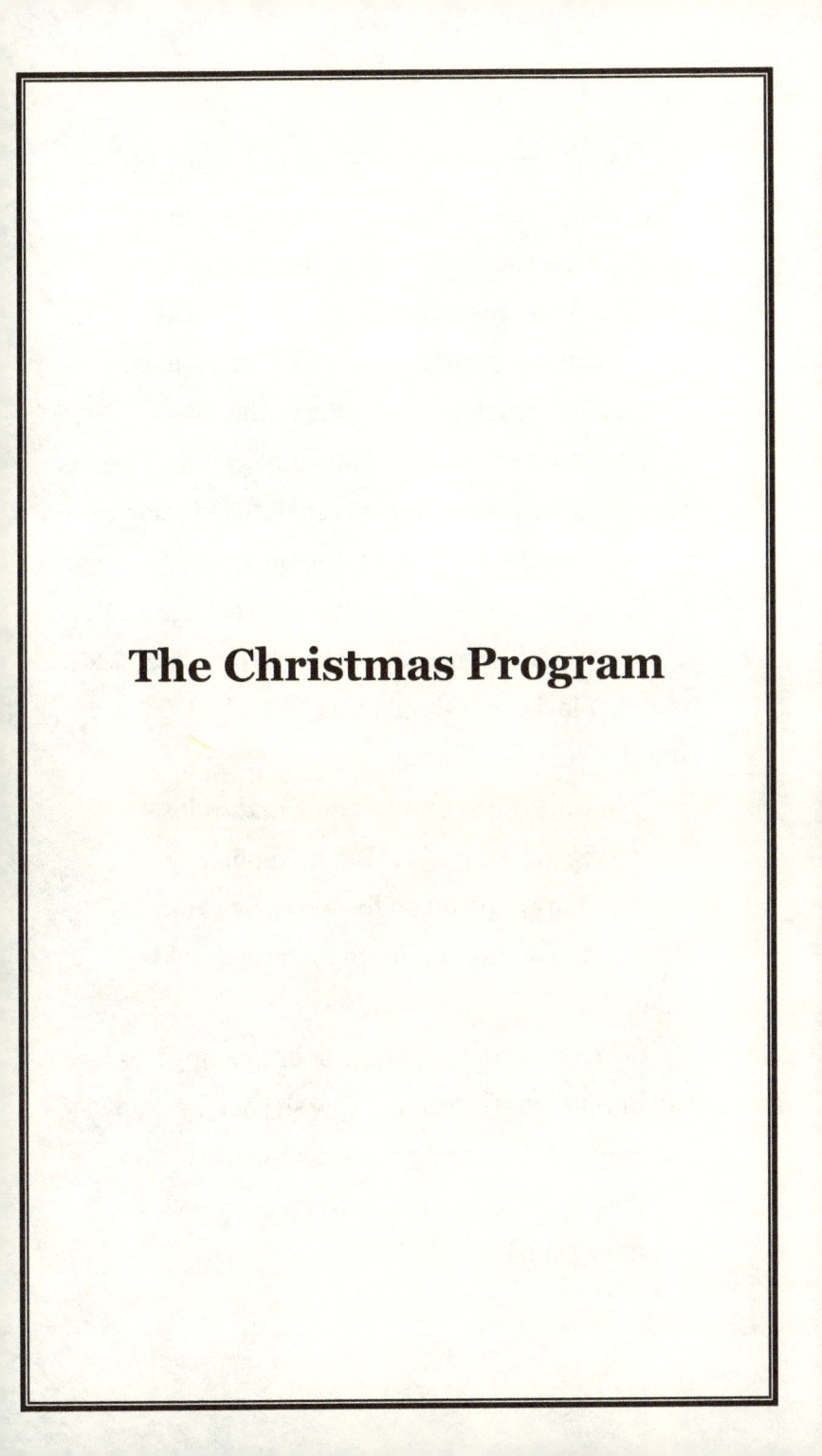

The Christmas Program

"Mom, can you fix my costume?" asked Liam who was panicking about his camel costume looking right for the Christmas program.

"I'm on it. It should be easy to fix," said Gracelyn as she grabbed her sewing kit to mend the camel hump that was falling to the side.

As Emma was helping hold the costume in place for her mom to sew, she said, "Glad I don't have to wear those silly costumes anymore."

"I can remember when you were his age and you wore an adorable snowflake costume. I still have it. Maybe you should wear it tonight," Gracelyn joked to Emma.

"No way! Keep that costume in the closet. I'm too big for it anyway," Emma replied.

"Ok, hurry up and go fix your hair. Your dad will be home in just a minute," Gracelyn told Emma.

The sound of the garage door opening was a sigh of relief for Gracelyn. Now she had backup and they could try and get out on time.

Walking into the house, Noah says, "Who broke the camel's back?"

"Funny. Can you help hold it up while I fix it?" Gracelyn asked as she put the finishing touch on Liam's costume.

Everyone was ready on time and they went to Liam's elementary school where the program was held.

"So, are you excited buddy?" Noah asked Liam.

"A little excited and a little nervous. I don't want to mess up," Liam replied.

"You'll be fine. You guys have been practicing this for weeks. You'll be the coolest camel on stage," Noah said as he was trying to give Liam confidence.

"I'm the only camel Dad," Liam said as he rolled his eyes.

They arrived at the school and people were pouring into the building. Everyone was jockeying for a good seat, so they could get a good picture of their child during the program. They dropped Liam off with his teacher and got a seat in the auditorium.

As they were waiting for the program to start, Noah started reading the program. He noticed half way through was Liam's name and he had been assigned a speaking part. The curtain rose up and the program began.

Noah and Gracelyn constantly kept smiling back at each other and laughing as the program went on. Noah was enjoying it so much and he still had Liam's part to look forward to. Liam walked out in his camel costume, adjusted the microphone, and spoke his part. He did such a wonderful job that Noah started tearing up. He was proud of his son. Noah could not fathom what it would have been like if he put work first that evening and missed this special moment. He was so glad he got to see his son perform that evening. Now he was looking forward to the Gingerbread Festival that was coming up this weekend.

Gingerbread Festival

Every year, except last year when Noah worked, Noah and his family would go to the annual Gingerbread Festival. It was one of their family's favorite holiday traditions. The festival was full of family friendly activities and everyone found something they enjoyed there. There was the gingerbread house making contest, a station where the kids would make gingerbread ornaments for their Christmas tree, musical entertainment on the stage, and the crowd favorite was a walk-thru gingerbread village. The village was nationally recognized in several travel magazines and websites.

The festival was taking place the weekend before Christmas. This year was going to be a challenge for Noah's family because of a packed weekend of other commitments. Both of the kids had basketball games, which were both out of town, and since this was the weekend before Christmas, Gracelyn wanted to finish up all the Christmas shopping.

The weekend was off to a whirlwind start.

"Dad, do you know where my basketball jersey is?" asked Emma.

"Don't forget I need my basketball aired up too," added Liam.

As he was trying to get ready himself, Noah shouted from his room, "Guys, why did we wait until the last minute to get our things in order? We knew all week we had games today and that this was going to be a busy weekend."

Noah took a pause and looked at himself in the mirror. Thinking back on his conversation with Sam, he reminded himself to just relax and put it all in perspective. Noah took a deep breath, smiled, and finished getting ready for the busy weekend ahead.

After the ball games were finished, they arrived at the festival. The kids were grinning ear to ear when they saw the gingerbread village. Noah rolled down the windows as they drove around looking for a place to park and the aroma of gingerbread quickly filled the inside of their car.

Closing her eyes and smiling, Gracelyn said "Just smell that wonderful scent. I love gingerbread. I can almost taste it."

Noah parked in a nearby spot and they all headed over to enjoy the festival.

The festival was packed. While it was a fantastic place to celebrate the holidays and had become a family tradition, the crowds could change your attitude in a heartbeat. Attendance had grown substantially over the years, especially with all the news coverage it was getting. Noah was determined that the crowds would not influence his mood.

"Watch where you're walking out of towner," a grumpy local said to someone who bumped him.

The person who actually was from another town apologized and continued to be amazed by all the gingerbread creations.

Witnessing the exchange of words, Noah went over to the grumpy gentleman, "Happy Holidays Mr. Walters. Are you enjoying the festival?"

"I was until that person about knocked me back into last Christmas. How rude of him," replied Mr. Walters.

Trying to calm him down, Noah replied, "Oh, I'm sure it was an accident. There's a lot to take in here. It's easy to get distracted and with the crowd accidental bumps are likely to occur."

Reluctant to agree, Mr. Walters replied, "Yeah, yeah. Well, it used to never be this crowded. Just ten years ago, you could actually take your time and look at the exhibits without fearing you'd be knocked over. Now I spend more time focusing on where to walk rather than enjoying what's on display."

Ceding to Mr. Walters' point, Noah was ready to move on and told Mr. Walters, "I see your point Mr. Walters. Just remember the big picture that while crowds may grow, you can still enjoy the great works of the festival and everyone is here to have a great time with their families. Try not to knock anyone down and enjoy the rest of your time here," as he smiled at Mr. Walters.

Mr. Walters got Noah's point and cautiously navigated his way through the traffic to the next exhibit.

It was a few minutes till 7 p.m. and the gingerbread house contest was getting ready to start.

"Hurry guys, we need to find a spot at the table to make our house," Gracelyn said as she quickly led the family to an open station.

"I wonder what kind of candy we'll have to decorate?" asked Liam.

"Probably similar to what we used a couple years ago," replied Emma.

"Yuck, that hard, cheap candy?" asked Liam.

"Keep in mind there's hundreds of people here and that candy worked great. It's colorful and looked nice on the gingerbread," replied Gracelyn.

They made it in time and away the contestants went. Gracelyn, the organizer in the family, had given each of them areas to focus on. Noah was in charge of stability. Meaning, he held the gingerbread pieces in place while Emma used frosting to secure everything in place. Liam was in charge of sorting the candy for him and Emma to decorate. Gracelyn gave herself the task of cutting out the gingerbread house pieces.

"It's caving in. It's caving in," screamed Emma, as all the walls were falling apart.

"You've got one job," Gracelyn said to Noah as she winked at him.

"I'm sorry. I think I'm squeezing the walls too hard. We've got plenty of time. I can fix this," Noah said confidently as he scrambled to keep the walls upright with icing all over his fingers.

The contest lasted for thirty minutes and the room was full of creative and colorful gingerbread houses. During those thirty minutes Noah and his family laughed so much. Liam kept eating the candy and Noah looked like he stuck his hands in a tub of frosting. After they finished they walked around and admired the rest of the houses. They laughed, were amazed, would talk about different designs, and had so much fun seeing all the other gingerbread creations together as a family.

When the evening was over they were each smiling so happily. Noah watched his kids as they kept talking about all the fun things they saw and did that night. It reminded him that traditions like this were important and he was so glad he made sure he did not let work interfere with the great memories his family made that night.

The Blitz

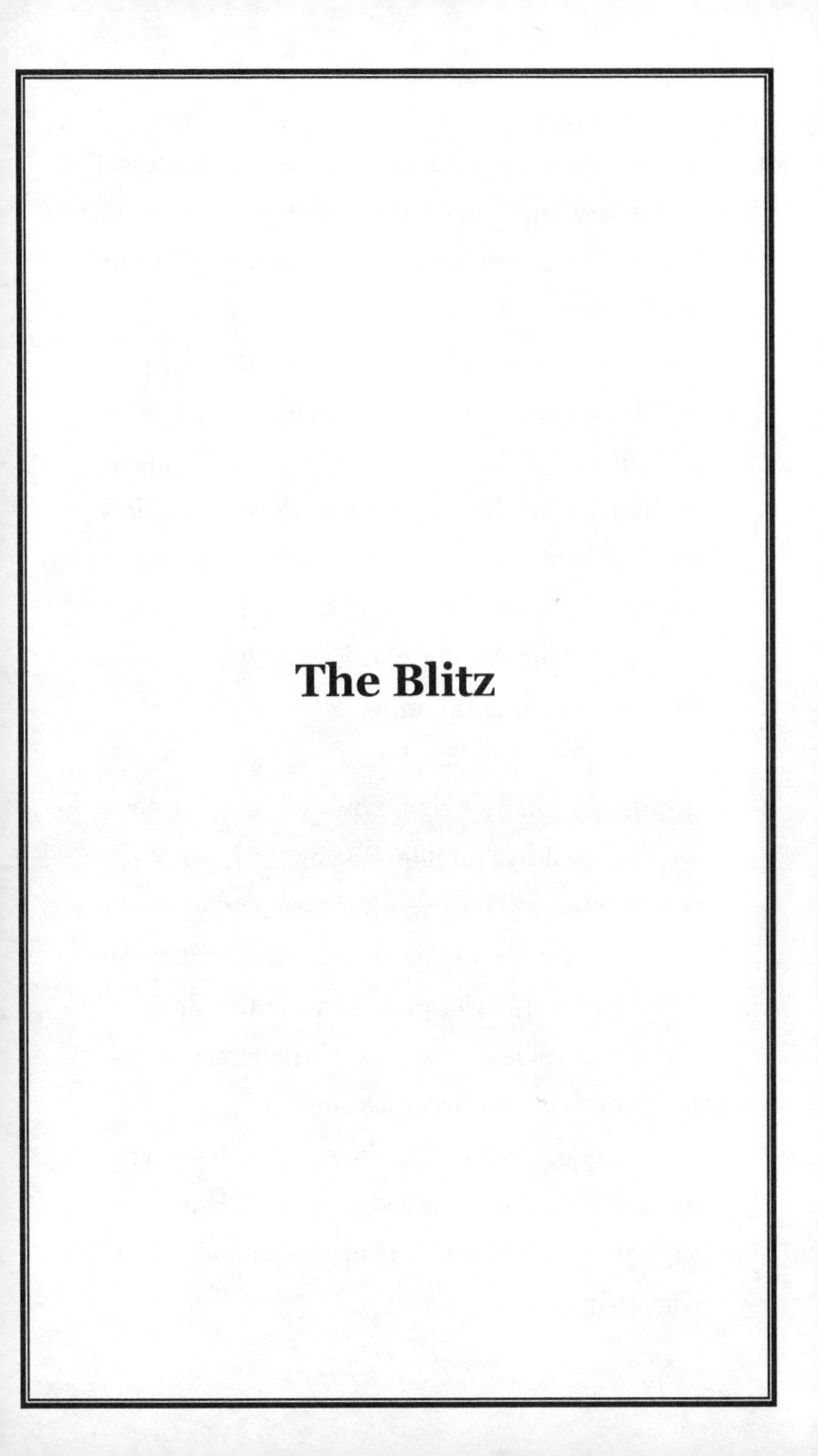

It was Friday, December 23, and Noah was trying to wrap things up at work before he went on Christmas break. His company was still open during Christmas, but Noah would use his vacation time to make sure he was off with his family. Since his company kept working, it would slow down a little, but the work would still pile up on him, leaving him something he would not look forward to at the start of the New Year. It was frustrating to know he would start the New Year already behind, but for now he would focus on the time off with his family.

"Yes, Mr. Jenkins. I am completing the acquisition analysis right now. I'll send it your way in about five minutes. Be on the lookout for it in your inbox shortly. I hope you and your family have a Merry Christmas," Noah said to one of the company's vice presidents on the phone. The vice president replied to Noah telling him he did not celebrate Christmas and Noah embarrassedly said, "Oh, I'm sorry, well you are missing out. I hope someday you decide to experience it." Noah hung up the phone and got back to his report.

Right before Noah sent the report to the vice president, Gracelyn texted him, "Don't forget to pick up the ingredients I need, plus the kids' stocking stuffer things. Oh, and be careful out there it's starting to snow." Noah had totally spaced his after work errands for Gracelyn, but it was almost Christmas break and he welcomed any task that came his way as long as it was not work related. In this case, the honey-dos were totally fine by him. Thankfully there was a grocery store a few blocks from his office that would carry everything he needed.

Like most Fridays, Noah was usually one of the last people to leave work. He put the finishing touches on the report for the vice president, hit send, and started shutting his computer down. Christmas break was about to begin and he was super excited. He was so anxious to go home and see his family he almost forgot the text his wife had sent him moments before. "Shucks, I almost forgot, got to pick up those things" as he rushed out of the building lobby. "Have a great Christmas, Bill!" he shouted to the building security guard.

As Noah pulled into the grocery store he was shocked to see the amount of cars in the parking lot. "You have got to be kidding me! I think everyone in the city is here." Noah parked in the back of the lot and briskly walked to the store.

As he made it through the bell ringers and dodged the waves of shopping carts coming his way, he made it in the door. It looked like the store had been hit by a storm, but all this chaos was not going to upset him. He had officially started his Christmas vacation!

"Almond bark. What the heck is almond bark?" he wondered. There was no available clerk in sight since they were all hands on deck at the checkout, so he took off to the candy isle.

"Almond bark sounds like a candy," as he looked top to bottom for this mystery ingredient. With the almond bark nowhere in sight, Noah headed to the cracker aisle. With his confidence in finding it dropping by the second, he told himself, "If I can't find it here, I'm going to have to find someone to help me."

After several minutes wasted, Noah saw a clerk, "Excuse me, can you help me find almond bark?"

"Sure, follow me, it's in with the baking items," replied the clerk.

Noah shook his head and realized that he should have asked Gracelyn or another customer. He grabbed the rest of the items on Gracelyn's list and headed up to the checkout lanes.

Noah approached the checkout lanes and could not believe that they were each about five to six customers deep. This was definitely one of those moments when Noah realized that the grocery home delivery services would have been a better choice. He patiently waited and when he was the second person in line is when the credit card system went down.

"Seriously?" he disappointedly said out loud.

"Christmas overload. Tis the season to be charging," said the customer in front of him.

Noah took a deep breath and remembered once more all the things Sam said. No more stress was going to ruin his Christmas spirit.

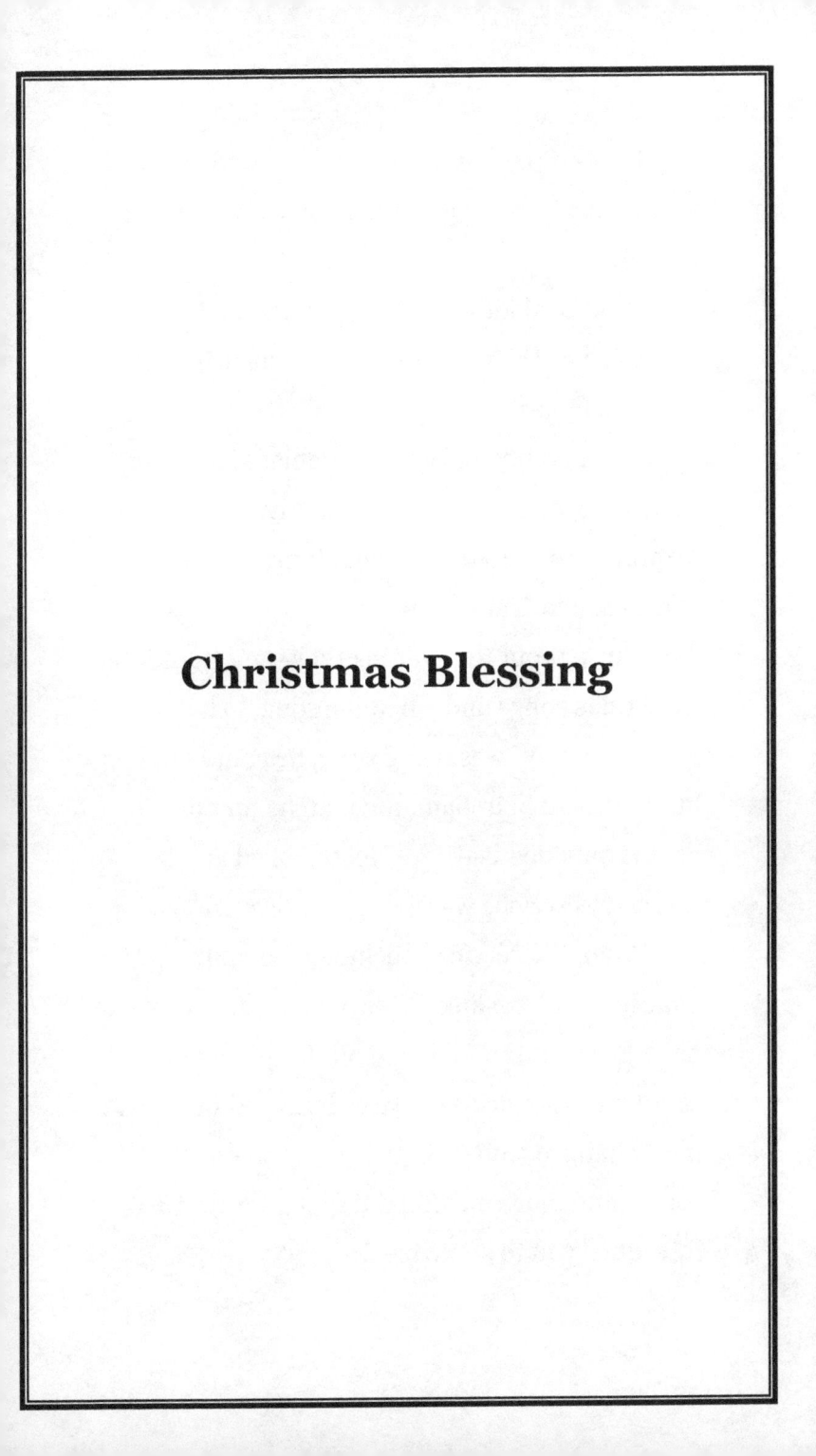

Christmas Blessing

It was 5 p.m. on Christmas Eve and Noah's family was attending candlelight service at their church.

"Daddy, daddy, my finger's melting," Liam screamed as the wax from the candle dripped onto his finger.

Noah grabbed his handkerchief and wiped Liam's finger off. "You're ok buddy. It's just wax dripping. Make sure you hold it up straight," he whispered to Liam.

Throughout the evening they sang traditional Christmas songs and when the song, "The Little Drummer Boy" was being sung, he could not help but to think about Sam, the man he met playing drums outside his work. Noah looked at his watch and service was just about over.

When the service concluded, he told Gracelyn and the kids, "I have an idea. I know we have this tradition of going out for pizza after candlelight service each year, but would you care if we changed things up this year and did something more meaningful first? I want to introduce you to someone."

With his family totally confused about what Noah had in store for that evening, he went to the ATM and then drove downtown to the restaurant where Sam worked. He remembered Sam telling him at lunch earlier that week that he would be working on Christmas Eve.

When they arrived at the restaurant, they saw Sam cooking back in the kitchen. He was singing Christmas songs as he set a plate on the counter and tapped the bell like it was cymbals on a drum set.

"Hey, Noah," said Sam as he waved from the window to the kitchen.

Noah waved back and sat down with his family at a table. Shortly after they ordered, Sam came out to greet them.

"What brings you and your family down here?" asked Sam while he shook Noah's hand.

"I wanted to introduce my family to you," Noah replied, "This is my wife Gracelyn, daughter Emma, and son Liam."

Excited to meet them, Sam shook all their hands and as he was shaking Liam's hand, "It's a pleasure to meet you all. Wow, what a firm handshake young man. Well done."

Anxious to tell his family about Sam, Noah said, "I wanted you to meet Sam. I met Sam a few weeks ago. He's an amazing drummer. The other day I met him again here working and we had a great conversation. He's a hard worker, brings joy to people's lives, and really has the right perspective on life," and he turns back to address Sam, "I wanted my family to meet someone special like you."

Embarrassed by Noah's kind words, Sam replied, "Aw, well thanks Noah. That's mighty nice of you to say that. I really think God connected us and it has been an honor to get to know you too my friend."

Both Sam and Noah gave each other hugs and Sam went back to his job, singing Christmas music along the way.

After they finished their meal, Noah asked the waitress if she had an envelope. She got him one from under the counter and he took money he just withdrew from the bank and put it in there. He then asked her to give it to Sam.

They all got up and waved goodbye as the waitress brought Sam the envelope.

"This is from that nice family," the waitress said.

Sam set down his spatula and towel and took the envelope. He looked at the envelope and it read, "To the man who brings everyone Joy! Have a blessed Christmas Sam!"

Sam opened it up and inside was $250. Noah had decided to give Sam half of his Christmas bonus. Sam pulled the money out of the envelope and looked up above.

He then pointed straight up and said, "Thank you Lord." The money came at a perfect time for the hard working and joy giving Sam. God had brought both of these men together to help each other out in different ways.

Full of Surprises

Noah and his family arrived home from Sam's restaurant and were getting settled in for Christmas Eve. Gracelyn was helping the kids prepare cookies and milk for Santa when Liam said, "Mom, don't forget the reindeer."

"What should we give them to eat buddy?" she asked.

"Cookies will just give them gas. You have to give them carrots," Liam told her.

Gracelyn and Emma burst out laughing.

"That's the first time I've ever heard that, but we do have some baby carrots in the fridge. I'll add them to the plate," said Gracelyn.

Gracelyn and the kids came back in to the living room where Noah was trying to start the fireplace when all of the sudden they heard a pounding sound outside.

Emma glanced out the window and in a scared voice said, "Dad, there's a big man outside doing something to our yard."

"Maybe that's Santa," Liam shouted.

Rushing over to the window, Noah looked out and realized who it was, "Oh, that's your

Uncle Michael. I'm not sure what he's up to, but I'll find out."

Noah went outside and saw a beautiful display in his front yard.

"Ho, Ho, Ho!" Michael said to Noah.

"Michael...did you make this?" Noah asked in amazement.

"I did. It's a gift for you guys, but especially for Gracelyn. I remembered at Thanksgiving time she said she wished she had an outdoor nativity set, so I decided to build her one," Michael proudly said.

"It's unbelievable. I'm so impressed and you did an amazing job," said Noah.

"Thanks. You remember that day you dropped the baseball home plate off for me to frame and you saw that guy over at my house? That was a friend who used to work with me at the coal mine. He was helping me with some of the wood cutting. I know it looked suspicious, but we just didn't want you to see what we were making," explained Michael.

In disbelief of the wonderful work of art Michael created, Noah said, "I'll admit, it did seem a little fishy that night. Thank you for this. I'm really proud of you."

Noah gave Michael a hug and then ran in to get Gracelyn and the kids so they could see the unexpected surprise.

"Merry Christmas Gracelyn!" said Michael.

"Oh my, gosh! You have got to be kidding me. Did you make this?" asked Gracelyn.

"Yep. I hope you like it. I had a little help, but I did most of it myself. I remember you saying you wish you had one, so...now you do," said Michael.

"It's absolutely perfect Michael. Better than I ever envisioned. Now I can say my Christmas decorations are complete. That's the best nativity set I've ever seen and I look forward to setting it out every Christmas. Thank you," Gracelyn said as she gave Michael a big hug, "Now let's get you inside where it's warm. Who wants some hot chocolate?"

Everyone smiled and went back into the house.

Noah had realized that he should not be too quick to judge and that the Holy Spirit had been working in some really amazing ways.

After Michael had delivered one unbelievable surprise, Noah decided exactly where the other half of his Christmas bonus should go.

"Merry Christmas Michael," Noah said as he handed Michael an envelope, "I know things will be a little tight with the layoff at work, but hopefully this will help you out until work picks back up again."

"Thanks Noah. You didn't have to do this. I was going to ask mom and dad for a little help, but now I won't have to. This will really help. Thank you," said Michael as he gave his little brother a hug.

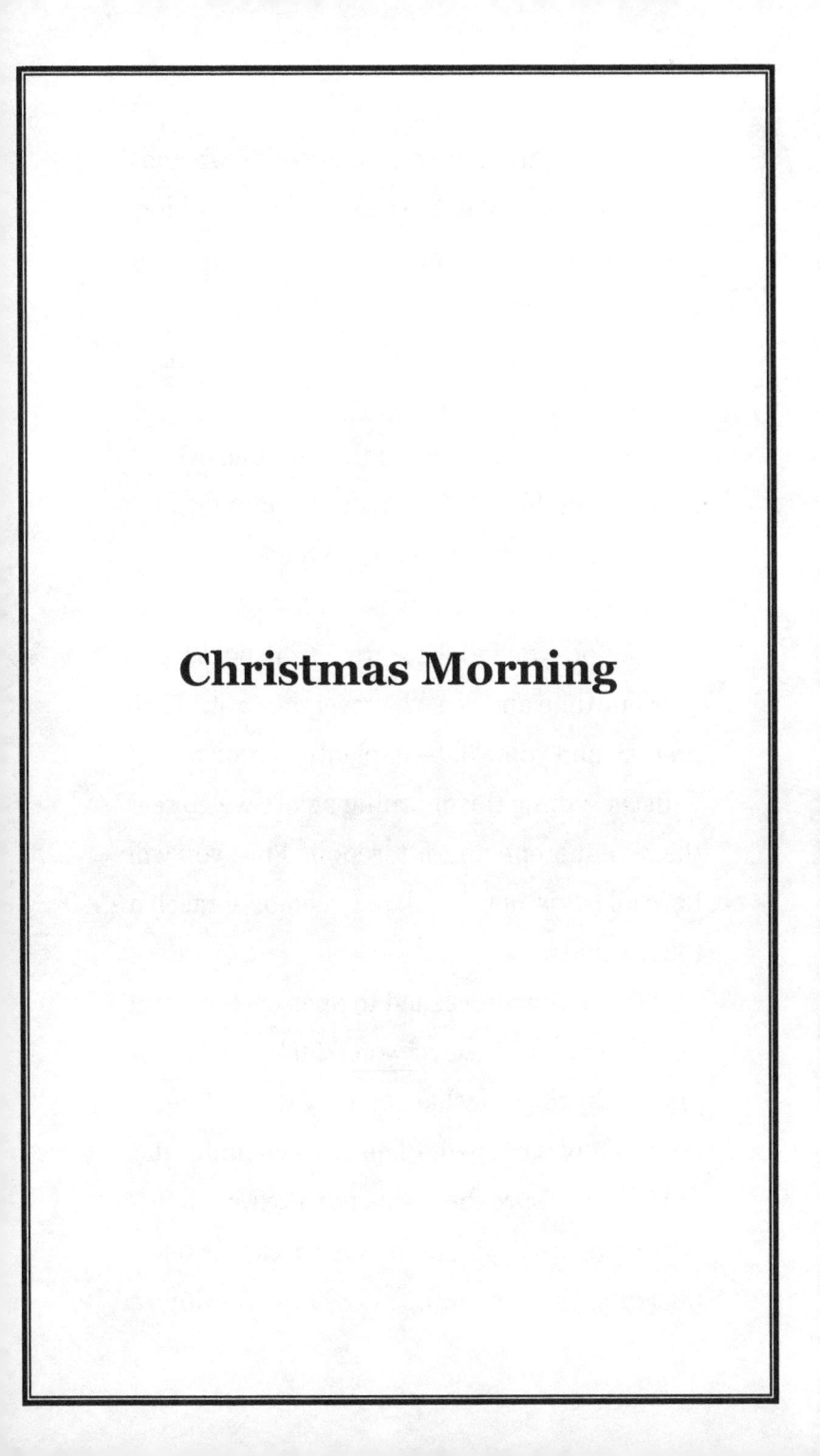

Christmas Morning

It was 5:30 in the morning and Noah and Gracelyn woke up to the sound of feet walking down the stairs. As they started to get up, they could hear the kids talking.

"Wow, look under the tree," Emma softly said to Liam.

"Yes! Santa made it. I thought I heard reindeer on the roof last night," Liam said.

Noah and Gracelyn put on their robes and slippers and headed downstairs.

"Before you kiddos start, let's make sure we take our time and see what everyone got. There's no rush and you will have plenty of time to play with everything this morning before we go see the grandparents this afternoon. Plus, you will have all Christmas break to play too," Gracelyn told the kids.

The family proceeded to open each present and Noah and Gracelyn would look at each other often, realizing how blessed they were. After every gift was opened, Liam crawled under the tree to make sure there was not anything left. He noticed tucked away in the very back was one final gift. The tag on the gift read, "To Emma &

Liam. Love, Santa." Not having a clue of what it may be, both of the children opened it to together.

After the first rip of wrapping paper revealed part of what was wrapped inside, Emma got excited and said, "Is that what I think it is?"

"It is, it is! The C.H.A.M.P. Robot!" Liam shouted with excitement. Both of the kids were so excited to get it.

"Looks like you both were officially on Santa's good list," Noah said to the kids.

As the kids started to play with the robot, Noah stepped out of the room.

"I'll go get some more batteries for the other toys," said Noah.

He arrived back in the room holding one more present for Gracelyn. It was a large flat square shaped gift. Gracelyn knew this year would finally not be anything jewelry related.

"Oh my, what could this be?" Gracelyn surprisingly said.

"It's just one more little gift I came up with," replied Noah.

Gracelyn took the present and opened it up. Tears of happiness flowed down her cheek when she saw that Noah had discovered the painting that had an impact on her years ago.

"This painting moved me too. I can understand why you fell in love with it. Let me tell you the story about how I got this," Noah said to Gracelyn.

"Is this the original painting?" she asked.

"It's not the original, but I was able to find it during my work trip to Knoxville. I took a picture of it, enlarged it, and got it framed. It belongs to a church in the Smoky Mountains and that is its home. If you look on the back, there is another picture of the painting beside a flag and on the other side a soldier. This was going to be a gift for him, a hero, and he didn't make it back from Iraq. I figured this would be the next best thing and someday I will show you the original painting that you saw years ago."

"This is great Noah. Thank you for going out of your way to do this. I'm impressed you remembered and thank you for doing this for me.

This is so special," Gracelyn said as she gave Noah a kiss.

"It was fun to go on a search for it. Because of that night I had an experience I will never forget," he said.

"What was that?" she asked.

"They had a food pantry at the church and they let me serve with them that night. It felt good to help others in their community who struggle with putting food on the table. That's something we take for granted. Seeing them help and show love to others gave me the desire to want to serve more. I plan on volunteering more and I would love for our family to find a way to serve together," Noah humbly said.

"I agree, hon. We should serve more. Maybe you can start by serving somewhere during your lunch break. I'll check with our church to see if they have any needs for our family to help with," Gracelyn happily said as she was glad to see the change in Noah's priorities.

During the rest of that Christmas Day, Noah and his family played games, watched movies, and enjoyed time together as a family. He realized just how blessed they were.

Putting Christmas in Perspective

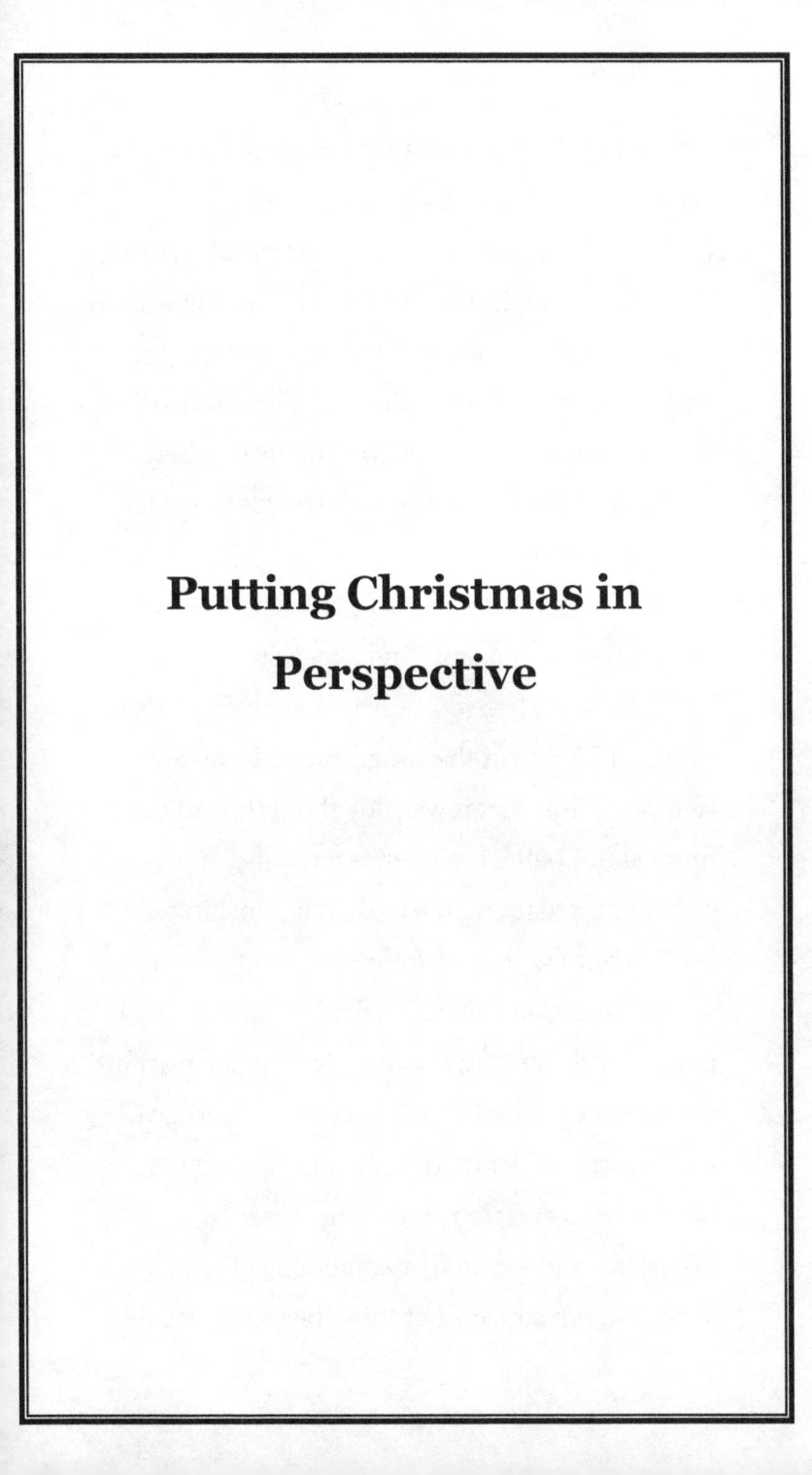

When you think of all the challenges we face each year at Christmas, it can be pretty overwhelming. In Noah's case, he raced against the clock giving himself the task of finding special Christmas gifts, and finding more time to spend with his family. During this time, he also worked at restoring the relationship with his brother. Everyone has their own set of stresses they face every holiday season.

Throughout the holidays Noah had encounters with people and experiences that helped him realize what Christmas time needs to be about. Being at the Gingerbread Festival reminded him that it was not about the gifts and more about being together as a family. It was also about regaining the close relationship he used to have with his brother.

When Noah volunteered at the church food pantry while looking for Gracelyn's painting it hit him that he needed to volunteer more and give back more. He learned from Sam that we are blessed with certain things, whether it be finances, time, talents, or something else special. When we recognize what those blessings are then that is when we should seek opportunities to put those gifts to work to help others.

Sam chose to share his time and talent of playing the drums with people so it would bring them joy. By sharing his Christmas bonus with Sam and Michael, Noah discovered that it was very rewarding to make an impact in someone else's life. Helping others was what needed to be a Christmas tradition, and also a yearlong priority for him and his family.

Another lesson Noah learned from Sam was about contentment. Noah put a lot of time and effort into gift giving, and he definitely surprised his family with some very special gifts. However, this season was an eye opener because he discovered how gifts and experiences given from the heart were much more cherished than any material gift bought in a store.

He also felt more thankful for his job. He had a great boss, a good team of employees, and generally liked what he did. He just could not allow work to consume him as much as he had.

As he put Christmas in "perspective", the most important thing of all was being thankful for God's blessings. God had blessed Noah's life in so many ways and Noah realized that. Up to this point, Noah took many of them for granted, but now he was getting his priorities in order. Instead of his career being the main objective, it would be honoring God and being there for his family that would be his priority.

Because of his conversation with Sam and time serving at the chapel in Gatlinburg, Noah decided to re-dedicate his life to Jesus and get baptized. By being a follower of Jesus Christ, he had already been saved by grace through his faith in Him. His goal now was to help make sure others would know how to receive this great gift too. Growing closer to God and family, along with helping others, would become the most rewarding things in Noah's life.

Sure Christmas time has those stressful moments, but isn't that what kind of makes Christmas time....well, Christmas? Face those holiday challenges head-on and embrace them when they occur. Enjoy every second of the season, and cherish every moment. Your kids will grow up, people will move, things change, and well, life happens. So for all the stress we may face during Christmas, do not let it distract you from what Christmas time is truly about and make sure you put it all in perspective, just like Sam said.

Thank you for reading the novella
"A Christmas of Surprises"!

I hope you enjoyed it and I would be honored if you reviewed it on Amazon and shared the book with others.

Blessings to you and your family!

Check out Derek Polen's other books:

A Dinosaur in the Sky

Hurry Up, Gus!

Moving to Bigcityopolis

A Money Saving Mindset:
40 Ways to Help You Save

Next Level Dad:
Bringing Faith and Fun to Fatherhood

About the Author

Derek Polen is a best-selling author of books that inspire and entertain. His work has been featured on SiriusXM radio, family magazines, podcasts and radio networks, and promoted by several social media influencers.

Having a passion for the business world, Derek has a Bachelor's degree in Marketing from Indiana State University and an M.B.A. from the University of Southern Indiana where he graduated with honors.

A lifelong learner, he also completed professional development programs from Duke, Harvard, M.I.T., and Northwestern. His professional experience includes leadership roles in Product Management and Supply Chain Management.

Derek likes spending time with his family and trying to find ways to help others and make a difference.

CPSIA information can be obtained
at www.ICGtesting.com
Printed in the USA
LVHW091818281119
638726LV00014B/2345/P